# The Doll in the Hall
## and Other Scary Stories

# Read more MISTER SHIVERS books!

# Mister Shivers

# The Doll in the Hall
## and Other Scary Stories

WRITTEN BY
**MAX BRALLIER**

ILLUSTRATED BY
**LETIZIA RUBEGNI**

**ACORN**™
SCHOLASTIC INC.

To librarians, teachers, and readers everywhere. —MB

To my amazing family and my wonderful parents
for always loving and supporting me. —LR

Library of Congress Cataloging-in-Publication Data

Names: Brallier, Max, author. | Rubegni, Letizia, illustrator. | Brallier, Max. Mister Shivers ; 3.
Title: The doll in the hall and other scary stories / written by Max Brallier ; illustrated by Letizia Rubegni.
Description: First edition. | New York : Acorn/Scholastic, 2021. | Series: Mister Shivers; 3 | Summary: The Clark children are Mia's first babysitting job, and everything is going fine until she sees a life-sized doll sitting in the hallway; a doll that was not there before, a doll that Mr. Clark knows nothing about, and whose eyes follow Mia—and that is only one of the five scary stories with unexpected twists that are included in this collection.
Identifiers: LCCN 2019054379 | ISBN 9781338615449 (paperback) | ISBN 9781338615456 (library binding) | ISBN 9781338615463 (ebook)
Subjects: LCSH: Dolls—Juvenile fiction. | Horror tales. | Children's stories, American. | CYAC: Horror stories. | Short stories. | LCGFT: Horror fiction. | Short stories.
Classification: LCC PZ7.B7356 Do 2021 | DDC 813.6 [Fic]—dc23
LC record available at https://lccn.loc.gov/2019054379

10 9 8 7 6 5 4 3 2 1                    21 22 23 24 25

Printed in China        62
First edition, January 2021
Edited by Katie Carella
Book design by Maria Mercado

# TABLE OF CONTENTS

Dear Reader,

I enjoy scary stories—like those in this book. (And like the one I escaped from.)

A box with a doll's dress on its top was left on my doorstep. Here is what I found inside:

- A rotten apple.
- A chewed-up carrot.
- Three baby teeth.
- Pumpkin seeds.

There was also a notebook in the box. Its pages were filled with scribbled handwriting. This note was taped to it:

PROMISE ME, MR. SHIVERS, THAT YOU WILL SHARE THESE STORIES. OR NEXT TIME YOU MIGHT NOT ESCAPE...

I keep my promises. And so, I must keep this one, too. Here I share those stories . . .

Mister Shivers

# THE DOLL IN THE HALL

**M**ia was babysitting for the first time.

She fed the Clark children dinner.

They watched a scary movie.

Then, she put the kids to bed.

Mia tiptoed back downstairs by herself.

That was when Mia first felt afraid...

She was not afraid because the house sat alone at the end of a long road.

She was not afraid because the wind was blowing through the trees. The wind sounded like laughter. **HEHEHEHE.**

But the **sound** was not the thing that scared Mia. The thing that scared Mia was something she had not seen before.

It was a life-sized doll.
It sat on a chair in the hall.

The doll's eyes seemed to follow Mia.

Its smile looked more **mean** than sweet.

And the dirt on its old clothes smelled fresh.

**RING!** Mia jumped. The phone was loud in the quiet house.

She grabbed the phone. It was
Mr. Clark. He was checking in.

"Everything is fine," Mia whispered.

She paused. She heard her own
breathing in the phone.

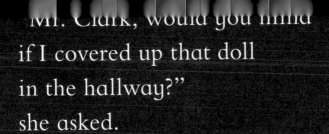

Mr. Clark, would you mind
if I covered up that doll
in the hallway?"
she asked.

Mr. Clark did not answer right away.

Then he spoke very slowly. He said,
"Mia, we don't have a doll
in our hallway . . ."

This time the sound did not come
from the wind. Or the trees.
It came from the doll.

# THE CAST

The worm poked its head out of an apple.

Danny looked up at the apple tree and saw the worm. He thought the worm was smiling at him. He didn't like it.

"I'll get you!" Danny yelled.

Danny climbed the tree. He crawled out on the branch. He reached up—

**CRACK!** The branch broke.

As Danny fell, he heard strange, high-pitched laughter. Then—

**WHAM!** Danny hit the ground.

He woke up at the hospital.

He was wearing a cast. It covered his arm from wrist to elbow.

"The skin under your cast might itch," the doctor warned.

And Danny's arm did itch.
**All the time.**

He couldn't think.

He couldn't sleep.

He begged his parents, "Help!"

Danny's parents took him
back to the doctor.

"Doctor, please take my cast off!"
cried Danny. "It's so itchy!"

The doctor shook his head. "I'm sorry.
Casts are itchy. That's normal."

The next day, Danny felt his skin **moving** beneath the cast.

"Mom! Dad!" cried Danny.
"I can't take it!"

"Your arm only feels itchy because it's healing," said Mom.

"The cast won't be on much longer," said Dad.

Finally, it was time to take off the cast.

**"Hurry!"** Danny begged.

The doctor began to cut the cast.
The saw was huge and shiny.
**GRRRRR-WRRZZZZ!**

"Faster!" shouted Danny.

The cast loosened. At last,
Danny pulled his arm free!

He started to thank the doctor—
but then he **screamed**!

His parents cried out.
The doctor fainted.

Worms covered his arm! Thousands of squiggly, squirming worms!

One worm looked up at Danny. This time, Danny was **sure** it was smiling.

# BRIGHT WHITE TEETH

Millie lived on a carrot farm.

A bowl of carrots sat on the dinner table. Millie did **not** like carrots.

Millie's mother said, "Eat up, Millie. Carrots are good for your eyes."

Her father added, "Rabbits eat carrots so they can run around at night."

"I want to see in the dark like the rabbits!" Millie said.

So she ate **all** the carrots.

After dinner, Millie snuck outside to test her new eyesight. It was dark.

She could not see anything. She needed to eat more carrots!

The dirt felt cool beneath Millie's feet.

Mille pulled a carrot from the ground.

And she ate it!
Then she ate another.

Millie ate a whole row of carrots.

But she **still** could not see in the dark.

Millie ate a second row of carrots.
And a third. And more!

But she **still** could not see in the dark.

There was only one row of carrots left.

Millie was very full. But she **really**
wanted to see in the dark
like the rabbits.

So, she ate the last row. And—

It worked!

"I can see in the dark!"
Millie said.

But Millie did not like what she saw.

Hungry rabbits stood in a circle around her.

Their mouths snapped open and shut.

They chanted, "You ate our carrots!
You ate our carrots!"

The rabbits crept closer and closer.

Millie saw hundreds of angry eyes
and hundreds of sharp teeth
shining in the darkness.

The last thing Millie ever saw
were bright white rabbit teeth.

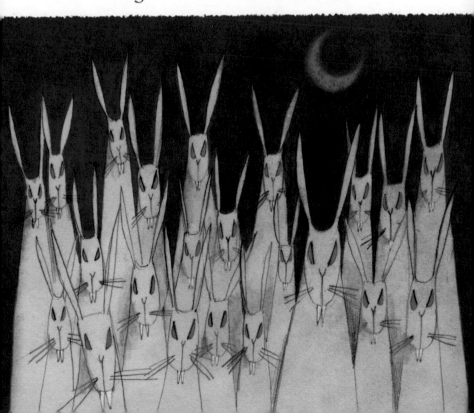

# THE JACK-O'-LANTERN

Halloween was Lila's favorite holiday.

She loved carving jack-o'-lanterns with her best friend, Willy. She loved trick-or-treating with her classmates.

But this year, Lila had no one
to enjoy Halloween with.

She had just moved to
a new town and a new school.

Lila carved a jack-o'-lantern. She took her time. She had no friends to catch up with.

She carefully carved the eyes.

She slowly made a nose.

Finally, she cut out a wide, smiling mouth.

Lila named the jack-o'-lantern "Willy."

"Hey, Willy," Lila said. "Why was
the jack-o'-lantern afraid to
cross the road?"

Willy seemed to watch Lila,
waiting for the punchline.

"It had no guts!" Lila said, laughing.

Willy seemed to laugh, too.

Lila took Willy trick-or-treating.
She told him more jokes—about new
neighbors and other trick-or-treaters.
Willy definitely smiled.

Willy was the perfect friend.
No fights over which house to visit next.
No fights over candy.

It was a good Halloween.

Lila wasn't ready to say goodbye
to Willy. So she kept him
in her bedroom.

Lila's parents tried to throw
Willy away.

"No!" begged Lila.

Then Willy began to rot.
Jack-o'-lanterns always rot.

Willy's eyes sunk
and his mouth
twisted.

And he began
to smell.

Lila knew it was time to say goodbye.
But she couldn't just dump Willy
in the trash.

So Lila dug a hole in her backyard.
She buried her only friend.

Next Halloween, Lila could not wait to go trick-or-treating.

Lila ran downstairs and told her parents, "I'm so happy it's Halloween! This year, I have **so many** friends to go trick-or-treating with."

Her parents smiled. They asked, "When are your friends coming over?"

"They're already here," Lila said.

Lila led her parents to a tree in their backyard. She pulled aside some overgrown branches.

A pumpkin patch grew there.
Each pumpkin was still on the vine.
And each pumpkin had a face—a
face like Willy's.

# BILLY SMILED

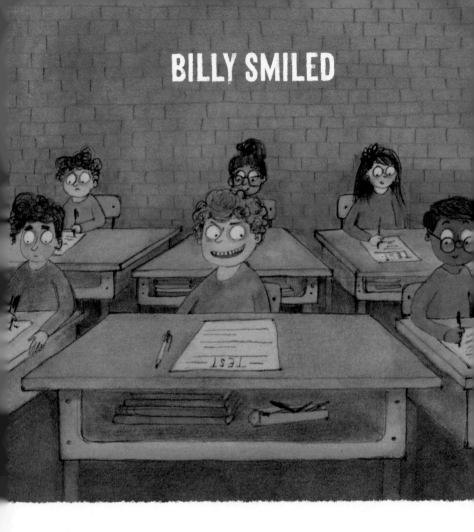

**B**illy was a cheater. He cheated at **everything**, and he never got caught.

Billy wanted a good grade on his math test. So he dropped his pencil on the floor.

Billy smiled when he got a perfect score.

Billy wanted to ride the fastest roller coaster. So he shoved cardboard into his shoes.

Billy smiled when he got away with it.

Billy wanted to see three movies for the price of one. So he snuck into the second and third movies.

Billy smiled.

He was **so** proud of his cheating that he started to laugh. Then—

**CRUNCH!** He bit a popcorn kernel. And—**OUCH!** He lost a tooth.

Billy looked at the kernel.
Then he looked at the tooth.

Suddenly he had a **great** idea!

Billy was going to cheat
the Tooth Fairy!

He brought his bag of
popcorn kernels home.

That night, he shook
the bag. The kernels
**sounded** just like teeth!

And in the dark,
the kernels **looked**
just like teeth.

Billy smiled and slipped the bag under
his pillow. He fell asleep dreaming
of how rich he would be.

In the morning, Billy reached beneath his pillow.

He felt paper. Money! He had cheated the Tooth Fairy!

But it was not money.
It was a note.

Billy frowned. And when he frowned, his mouth felt **weird**.

He hurried to the mirror.

All his teeth were gone. They had been replaced with rotten popcorn kernels.

Billy never smiled again.

# ABOUT THE CREATORS

**MAX BRALLIER** is the *New York Times* and *USA Today* bestselling author of more than thirty books including The Last Kids on Earth series, the Eerie Elementary series, and the Galactic Hot Dogs series. Max lives in New York with his wife and daughter.

**LETIZIA RUBEGNI** is a children's book illustrator. At an early age, she fell in love with storytelling through pictures. She carries her red sketch pad everywhere she goes to capture any interesting ideas. She lives in Tuscany, Italy.

# YOU CAN DRAW A RABBIT!

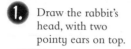

**1.** Draw the rabbit's head, with two pointy ears on top.

**2.** Add a nose. Draw a line from the nose straight down to the mouth.

**3.** Draw two eyes.

**4.** Draw a body, one arm, one leg, and two feet.

**5.** Draw the other arm and leg. Add details to the ears and belly. Add a tail. Don't forget two sharp fangs!

**6.** Color in your drawing!

# WHAT'S YOUR STORY?

The rabbits are mad at Millie for eating the carrots.
The story in this book ends with rabbits all around Millie
Imagine what happens next.
Do **you** think Millie gets away?
Write and draw your own scary story!